I0692479

British Museum, Alexander S. Murray

Terracotta Sarcophagi

Greek and Etruscan in the British Museum

British Museum, Alexander S. Murray

Terracotta Sarcophagi
Greek and Etruscan in the British Museum

ISBN/EAN: 9783337386917

Printed in Europe, USA, Canada, Australia, Japan

Cover: Foto ©Andreas Hilbeck / pixelio.de

More available books at **www.hansebooks.com**

TERRACOTTA SARCOPHAGI

GREEK AND ETRUSCAN

IN THE

BRITISH MUSEUM

BY

A. S. MURRAY, LL.D., F.S.A.
Keeper of Greek and Roman Antiquities

LONDON:

PRINTED BY ORDER OF THE TRUSTEES
AND SOLD AT THE BRITISH MUSEUM

AND BY LONGMANS AND CO, 39 PATERNOSTER ROW
BERNARD QUARITCH, 15 PICCADILLY; ASHER AND CO, 13 BEDFORD STREET, COVENT GARDEN
KEGAN PAUL, TRENCH, TRÜBNER AND CO, PATERNOSTER HOUSE, CHARING CROSS ROAD
AND HENRY FROWDE, OXFORD UNIVERSITY PRESS WAREHOUSE, AMEN CORNER

1898

[All rights reserved]

SARCOPHAGUS FROM CLAZOMENÆ.

Pls. I.—VII.

I N the early records of painting in Asia Minor we have been accustomed to read of a *Battle or Destruction of the Magnesians* painted by Bularchos,[1] a *Fight at the Ships* by Calliphon of Samos,[2] and a *Passage of the Army of Darius over the Bosporos*, painted at the instance of Mandrocles of Samos, as a memorial of the bridge he had constructed for Darius.[3] In the records of sculpture we know the details of the Throne of Apollo at Amyclæ by Bathycles of Magnesia, with which, because of its strongly Ionian affinities, we associate the famous chest of Kypselos. In legendary times we are told of Helena embroidering scenes of the Trojan war as they transpired before her eyes.[4] Homer, in his description of the Shield of Achilles, gives us an elaborate account of the work of the divine artificer, Hephæstos. From these actual or legendary statements we have been led to expect two things as characteristic of the early art of Asia Minor : first, compositions in which a multitude of figures were engaged ; and secondly, an occasional representation of actual, historical events. It would seem that both these expectations are realised in a striking manner by the sarcophagus from Clazomenæ recently acquired by the British Museum. The illustrations speak for themselves as to the multitude of figures. Nor can anyone doubt that the scene in which a horde of barbarians (Pl. I.) sweep down their Greek opponents is other than a historical picture of one of those invasions of Cimmerians into Asia Minor which Herodotus records.[5] It is not a battle scene in the ordinary sense, where two sides are more or less evenly opposed. It is a raid, *ἐξ ἐπιδρομῆς*

---

[1] Pliny, vii. 126 and xxxv. 55.

[2] Pausanias, v. 19, 1. *Cf.* x. 26, 2, where he again mentions the picture by Calliphon which was to be seen in the temple of Artemis at Ephesus. In the former passage he describes the picture as the *Fight at the Ships* (*Iliad*, xiii.), but in the second he mentions the arming of Patroclos (*Iliad*, xvi.) as having been represented in the picture. Robert, *Iliupersis des Polygnot*, p. 24, considers these two passages as taken from Polemo.

[3] Herodotus, iv. 88.

[4] *Iliad*, iii. 125.

[5] i. 15, an invasion of Cimmerians in the time of Ardys, the successor of Gyges, in which Sardis was captured, except the acropolis ; i. 16, Alyattes,

the second in succession after Ardys, expelled the Cimmerians from Asia Minor and invaded Clazomenæ ; i. 6, describes the invasion of the Cimmerians, which took place before the time of Crœsus, as not involving the destruction of cities, but as being *ἐξ ἐπιδρομῆς ἁρπαγή*. The capture of Sardis is attested also by Strabo, xiii. 627, where he quotes Callisthenes, and he again the poet Callinos, as the original authority ; also xiv. 647, where in addition he records the total destruction of Magnesia by the Cimmerians at some date between the poets Callinos and Archilochos ; in i. 20, Strabo seems to have convinced himself that an inroad of Cimmerians into Asia Minor had occurred as early as the time of Homer, or a little before. For examples of Scythian costume, see *Antiquités du Bosphore Cimmérien*, pl. 33.

ἁρπαγή, as Herodotus says expressly, in which the Cimmerians appear suddenly on horseback, sitting well back on their horses, striking down their enemies with huge swords, and sweeping across the field from one end to the other. It may be thought that in costume and horsemanship these barbarians do not differ in a sufficiently marked degree from the Persians on the frieze of the Nikè temple at Athens to warrant our identification of them as absolutely Cimmerians. But the differences, such as the use of a huge sword to strike down with, the characteristically Scythian head-gear, the accompaniment of dogs of war, and the wild rush of the movement, show that we have here to do with a barbarous people and not with Persians.

A few years ago the sarcophagi of Clazomenæ had suggested to the present writer a possible explanation of the statement of Pliny that the Magnesian picture of Bularchos had been purchased for its weight in gold by Candaules, the King of Lydia. It seemed that a picture painted on a slab of terra-cotta in the manner of the sarcophagi would under the circumstances have realised a price worthy of a Lydian king.[1] Since then M. Salomon Reinach[2] has taken a bolder step with the view of directly connecting the picture of Bularchos with particular scenes on the sarcophagi. Observing that there were to be seen on the sarcophagi occasionally warriors accompanied by dogs, he produced certain passages of ancient writers which showed that the Magnesians had in fact employed dogs of war.[3] It was a reasonable inference that the warriors accompanied by dogs on the sarcophagi were Magnesians. But his argument would have been more conclusive if he could have shown that the Magnesians, alone in Asia Minor, had used dogs for this service. Pliny[4] ascribes the same practice to the Colophonians, associating them in this respect with the Castabalenses of Cappadocia. We know that the Celtic peoples made liberal use of dogs in war,[5] and the evidence of our new sarcophagus would go to show that this usage had been more or less general in Asia Minor. Add to this the statement of Polyænus[6] that Alyattes had employed powerful dogs in his final defeat of the Cimmerians. Nor is this surprising when we see the great Asiatic goddess Cybele employing a yoke of lions to tear down her enemies, as in the frieze of Knidos (?) at Delphi. In the reliefs on our large terra-cotta sarcophagus from Cære one of the warriors is assisted by a lion (Pl. IX.). We are told that in the name Candaules, the first syllable is equal to *canis*, dog, and in a fragment of Hipponax κυνάγχα, an epithet of Hermes, is explained as equivalent to Κανδαῦλα in the Maeonian tongue.[7]

The object of M. Reinach was to prove that the picture of Bularchos had represented a battle, *prælium* (as Pliny says in one passage), and not a destruction, *exitium* (as he says in another). But whatever the truth of the matter

[1] *Handbook of Greek Archaeology*, p. 358. It is there suggested that the origin of painting on terra-cotta panels was to be traced to Asia Minor, and that the practice had thence passed to Corinth and Etruria.

[2] *Études Grecques*, 1895, p. 161. fol.

[3] Aelian, *de Nat. Animal.* vii. 38, and *Hist. Var.* xiv. 46; *Pollux*, v. 5, 47.

[4] viii. 143. It is true that this passage of Pliny corresponds, as far as it goes, to that of Aelian (*Hist. Var.* xiv. 46), quoted by M. Reinach, and it is possible, no doubt, that Aelian may be the better source of the two. This passage of Pliny was pointed out to me by Mr. Hill, of the Coin Department in the British Museum.

[5] Strabo, iv. p. 200.

[6] *Strat.* vii. 2, 1.

[7] Bergk, *Poet. Lyr. Gr.*[4] ii., p. 460.

may be, it is clear from Strabo (xiv. 647) that the Magnesian disaster was a subject of contention, on which he himself had made up his mind to the effect that it had taken place in the interval between the dates of the two poets Callinos and Archilochos. The passage from Athenæus,[1] quoted by M. Reinach, seems to be at variance with Strabo, since it gives Callinos as well as Archilochos as an authority for the ruin of the Magnesians. There may have been numerous raids of Cimmerians on Greek cities in Asia Minor, and there may have been many painters who painted these raids, but at present we only know as a fact the raids on Sardis, Magnesia, and Ephesus, the last mentioned having been disastrous to the barbarians.[2]

Leaving the relationship between the sarcophagi and the painting of Bularchos as perhaps uncertain, we may compare next the work of another Asia Minor artist,

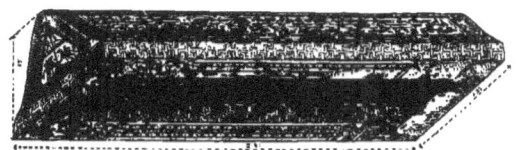

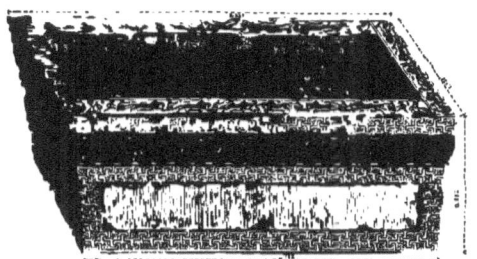

FIG. 1.—GENERAL VIEW.

Bathycles of Magnesia, whose extensive series of reliefs on the throne of Apollo at Amyclæ Pausanias[3] has described. Allowing for the great difference in the task that was set before Bathycles, and not expecting much community of subject, we can yet conceive that his Sphinxes, panther, and lioness may have fairly resembled in artistic type the Sphinxes and other animals on our new sarcophagus. But more to our purpose is his scene of the funeral games held by Acastos on the death of his father Pelias, because on our new sarcophagus perhaps the most prominent feature is the repetition of what I believe to be funeral games, ἆθλα or ἀγῶνις. It is true that in this instance Pausanias gives us no details, but he is more explicit in his description

---

[1] xii. 525': 'Απώλοντο δὲ καὶ Μάγνητες οἱ πρὸς τῷ Μαιάνδρῳ διὰ τὸ πλέον ἀνεθῆναι, ὥς φησι Καλλῖνος ἐν τοῖς ἐλεγείοις καὶ 'Αρχίλοχος ἑάλωσαν γὰρ ὑπὸ τῶν 'Εφεσίων. This excess of luxury which led to the ruin of Magnesia is referred to also by Theognis, 603 (Bergk).

[2] Callimachus, *Hymn to Artemis*, 251 fol.
[3] iii. 18, 9.

4

of the same contest (ἀγὼν ὁ ἐπὶ Πελίᾳ) on the *larnax* of Kypselos,[1] and as this famous work with its multitude of figures is now generally held to have preserved many elements of Ionian art, we may fairly take it into account here, the more so since our new sarcophagus may also be properly called a *larnax*. In passing I may suggest that it might be a satisfactory explanation of the escape of the infant Kypselos, if we could suppose him to have been hid in an urn or sarcophagus.

At this point it may be convenient to indicate briefly the position of the various

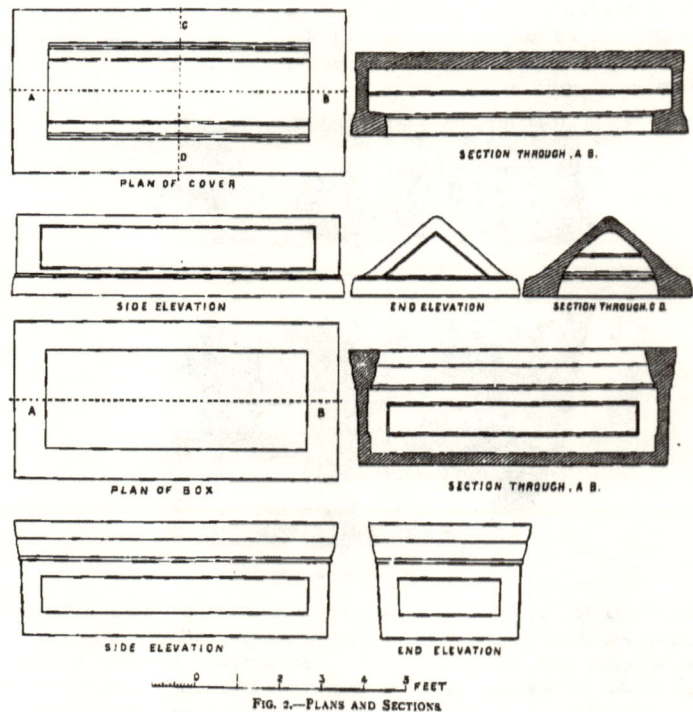

PLAN OF COVER

SECTION THROUGH A B.

SIDE ELEVATION

END ELEVATION

SECTION THROUGH C D

PLAN OF BOX

SECTION THROUGH A B.

SIDE ELEVATION

END ELEVATION

FIG. 2.—PLANS AND SECTIONS.

scenes on our sarcophagus (see Fig. 1). On the cover are four bands, two on each side, running parallel with each other; the better preserved side is given in Pl. I. The other side of the cover, now much injured, appears under Fig. 3. The body or box of the sarcophagus has four bands on the interior, two of them on the long sides (Pls. II.–III.), and two on the short ends (Pls. IV.–V.). On the upper edge of the body or box are chariot races (Pl. VI.), and on the under edge of the cover are

[1] Pausanias, v. 17, 4.

scenes of combat, groups of Dolon, Sphinxes and Harpies (Pl. VII.). The ends of the cover are shown in Figs. 4–5.

Beginning with the representation of funeral games on the long sides of the sarcophagus (Pls. II., III.), we find the central group consisting of two combatants with the spear, like Ajax and Diomede at the funeral games of Patroclos,[1] but having a youth playing on flutes between them. Corresponding to this group, we observe on the *larnax* of Kypselos Admetos and Mopsos boxing, with a man standing between them playing on the flutes, ἐν μίσῳ δὲ αὐτῶν ἀνὴρ ἐστηκὼς ἐπαυλεῖ. The whole band, on Pl. II., repeated on Pl. III., is clearly one of mimic war, and this is the more apparent when we are told by Pausanias in connection with the chariot race on the Kypsele that there was a *woman* playing on the flutes, he having obviously misunderstood the official costume of a flute player on such occasions. It has been suggested by Benndorf that in this instance the flute player had been dressed as a woman or girl, and his view has been rightly accepted. But we may venture to modify it so far as to say that the flute player may only have had the head-dress of a girl. That would have been enough to put Pausanias wrong and would bring the larnax of Kypselos into direct relationship with our new sarcophagus. In any case, the group on the sarcophagus disposes of the view of Mr. Stuart Jones that the flute player on the Kypsele must have been represented *en face*.[2]

On each side of the central group are two bigæ (συνωρίδες) ready for the race. Between each pair of bigæ is a youth dancing and shaking the *crotala* to excite the horses, while beside each biga stands a warrior holding up a whip to the driver, apparently as a signal for the start.[3] We do not remember having ever seen this motive before, but we feel sure that the handing up of the whip is an artistic indication that the race was about to commence. Obviously these groups on Pls. II.-III. do not answer to the chariot race on the Kypsele, where the bigæ are in full course and the prizes are set out on view. For that we shall find a better parallel on the sarcophagus presently. Meantime it may be suggested that what had puzzled Pausanias and the interpreters at Olympia in explaining the third band on the Kypsele was just some such scene as that on Pls. II.-III. What they saw was two bodies of armed men approaching each other, but instead of fighting, these armed men seemed to recognise and salute each other. So far as we know, no attempt has ever been made to explain this curious and striking passage of Pausanias, nor do we say that our two bands illustrate it so fully as could be wished. Yet we cannot help thinking that, had Pausanias seen on the Kypsele a representation of this kind, he would very probably have found himself in the very dilemma which he describes. It may seem strange no doubt that the actual chariot race, prizes and all, should be given on the first band of the Kypsele, while what appears like an earlier stage of the games does not come on till the third band. But on our sarcophagus we have much the same thing. On Pls. II.-III., as has been said, we see a preliminary stage of the contest, while on Pl. VI. the chariot race is in full swing, with the prizes set out at the ends.

---

[1] *Iliad*, xxiii. 798.
[2] *Hellenic Journal*, xiv. p. 67.
[3] Soph. *Electr.* 711, the chariot race was started by a trumpet χαλκῆς ὑπαὶ σάλπιγγος ἦξαν. In *Iliad*, xxiii. 362, the start is indicated by raising the whip and shaking the reins.

As regards Pl. VI., it may here be observed that in the centre, where the two sets of competing chariots appear to meet, stands a figure with raised hand, as if to warn the drivers. Clearly this figure is an ordinary mortal. In the one case he wears the regular helmet, and in the other the close cap with tresses escaping at the crown like the charioteers, and is in fact identical with the figure similarly placed on the Constantinople sarcophagus.[1] It will be remembered that at the games of Patroclos, Achilles erected a goal for the chariot race and placed Phœnix beside it to "observe the courses and bring him a true report."[2] These two figures may, we think, be taken as representatives of the part played by Phœnix. On one of the Paris sarcophagi we see a winged and draped female occupying this position, and warning the drivers with her hands and look. But we cannot regard her with M. Joubin[3] as a Nikè. She is rather a personification of an action usually performed by mortals. It will be noticed that on the last chariot in each set of competitors an armed man appears stepping up, whatever that may signify.

As regards the prizes, it will be observed that on the top of an Ionic column is placed a lebes—a characteristic prize vase—the effect being as if we had before us a combination of the Ionic and Doric capitals, the lebes representing the Doric echinus. Against the column rests a shield. The strangest thing, however, is that at the other side of the column appears a slight nude figure leaning on a staff, with knees bent as if to indicate dejection. So insignificant a figure cannot be a spectator, still less a judge of the games. We had thought of the female captive who was given as part of the prize for the chariot race at the funeral games of Patroclos,[4] and had supposed that in other circumstances a male captive may equally have been part of the prize. But remembering that at the death of Achilles the Greeks made a tumulus for him, and held an *agon* in which his arms were contended for by Odysseus and Ajax,[5] we now think it more probable that the column is meant to indicate the tomb from which the race started, while the shield would be that of the deceased set out as a prize. As the association of *eidola* with tombs is an accepted fact, it may be suggested that the nude, insignificant, dejected figure leaning on his staff and looking anxiously round may be the *eidolon* or shade of the deceased, in whose honour the games were held, the column indicating his tomb. The fact that this figure leans on a staff indicates a degree of dignity incompatible with the position of a captive or slave. His being nude may be at variance with what we know for certain of *eidola*,[6] but if Loeschcke is right in regarding the nude figure on a fragment of another Clazomenæ sarcophagus as an *eidolon*,[7] the difficulty would be removed. In any case we cannot forget that Æschylus, in the Persæ (609-681), makes the shade of Darius rise from his tomb at the offerings and hymns of Atossa and her friends.

[1] *Études Grecques*, 1895, pl. facing p. 161.

[2] *Iliad*, xxiii. 358; cf. Soph. *Electr.*, 709: στάντες δ᾽δθ᾽ αὐτοὺς οἱ τεταγμένοι βραβῆς, κ.τ.λ.

[3] *Bull. Corr. Hell.*, 1895, pl. 1, p. 69, fol.

[4] *Iliad*, xxiii. 259, 262.

[5] *Aethiopis* (Kinkel, *Epic. Gr. Frag.* p. 34). In the *Iliad*, xxiii. 798, Achilles sets forth the spear, shield, and helmet of Sarpedon as the prize of skill in the use of the spear.

[6] The *eidolon* of Patroclos appears in Gerhard, *A. V.* iii. pls. 198-199, as a diminutive armed figure hovering above his tumulus. The *eidolon* of Polydoros, who speaks the prologue to the Hecuba of Euripides, had not yet a tomb.

[7] *Aus der Unterwelt* (Dorpat-Programm), p. 5. *Bull. Corr. Hell.* 1895, pl. 1, p. 71.

On the Kypsele we are told of the combat of Ajax and Hector after the challenge, πρόκλησις, with the remark that between the combatants stood Eris, "most ill-favoured of aspect, resembling the Eris in a painting of the *Battle at the Ships*, by Calliphon of Samos, which was to be seen in the temple of Artemis at Ephesus." But as there is no reference to Eris in the *Battle at the Ships*, in *Iliad*, xiii., nor in the challenge of Ajax and Hector (*Iliad*, vii.), Calliphon must have introduced her from some source other than the Iliad, and in any case it does not necessarily follow that he had placed his Eris directly between the two combatants, though the comparison of Pausanias and not a few representations on archaic vases would almost prove so much. On one of the Clazomenæ sarcophagi, as already said, stands a winged female figure between the chariots who has been identified as Eris or Nikè.[1]

Let us take next the Doloneia as represented on the upper band of Pl. I., and in two simple groups on the lower face of the cover (Pl. VII.), a subject which has already been made familiar by the Berlin sarcophagus.[2] In Pl. I. we have a striking variation of the theme. On each side of the central group of Dolon is a set of racing bigæ approaching the centre, in contrast to the Berlin sarcophagus, where a winged personification of the Homeric kind steps into her chariot to drive away from the centre. Whatever the explanation of that figure may ultimately be, it would almost seem from our sarcophagus that the Doloneia, though in the Iliad it is merely a remarkable episode, must have originally, in some pre-Homeric lay, included funeral games on the death of Dolon. Be this as it may, we have in the winged figures which fly above each chariot a type of being which deserves special consideration.

Beginning with the first of these winged figures on the left of Pl. I. (upper band), we are at once struck with its resemblance, as an artistic conception, to these nude flying beings which occur on the early red-figure vases, as on our Kylix E. 13, and under the name of Eros continue to be represented on Greek vases to the end, with characteristic modifications as time went on. No wonder: it is a very beautiful conception. We can hardly be wrong in regarding the figure on our sarcophagus as the prototype of the others. But we must take into account also the other figures which fly above the chariots. It will be seen that one of them holds a branch, apparently of olive, which would suggest Nikè. But these figures are nude and cannot be Nikæ. They would better represent *Agon*, the spirit of contest. On the other hand, if we look to strictly archaic art for a comparison, we shall, perhaps, find it best in those flying figures which occur on vases of the so-called Cyrene fabric, particularly on two kylikes, on which we see a horseman on a large horse[3] attended by one of these winged beings. In one case the flying figure holds out a wreath, and this has led to its identification as Nikè, especially so since the short chiton was suggestive of a female. But on our well-known kylix from Naucratis,[4] figures, otherwise identical

---

[1] The vase in Gerhard, *A. V.* iii. 199, gives one of these winged, female figures approaching the chariot of Achilles to which Hector is bound beside the tumulus of Patroclos. She is there inscribed as ΚΟΝΙΣΟΣ (= *Konisalos*), and is supposed to per- sonify the dust with which the body of Hector was to be besmirched (*Iliad*, xxii. 401 ; xxiv. 17).

[2] *Ant. Denkmäler*, i. pl. 44.

Arch. Zeit. 1881, pl. 13, figs. 2—3.

[4] *Naucratis*, i. pl. 8.

with these, are either bearded or beardless, so that we may fairly regard the two winged beings attending the two horsemen on the kylikes as male. It has been suggested that they were *eidola* of deceased persons.[1] But, whether that is right or wrong, the suggestion would not apply to the chariot race on Pl. I. of our sarcophagus. These cannot all be "spirits from the vasty deep," even though the contest took place at funeral games. Possibly they are personifications of the games (*Agon*), and, as such, must rank among the numerous other personifications which fill the air of archaic Greece, like the *Konisalos*, already mentioned, who personified the besmirching of Hector's body.

In matters of armour and costume the sarcophagus raises some new questions. On sarcophagi from Clazomenæ two types of helmet had been previously remarked on. The one was noticeable for the sort of hook rising above the forehead, as on one of our fragmentary vases from Defenneh. Of this there is no example on our new sarcophagus. The other type was characterised by having the crown of the helmet formed of the skin of a bull's head, horns and ears included, while the lower part was painted purple to indicate bronze. This type is very frequent on our sarcophagus. It reminds us of a fragment of Choerilos, the Samian poet, where he describes the Solymi in the army of Xerxes as wearing on their heads the skin of a horse's face flayed and smoked.[2] Apparently the early Greeks had not had the experience of an enemy who struck downward with a great sword like the Cimmerians on our sarcophagus, and accordingly were free to treat the crown of the helmet more as an ornament than a protection. The crest is common to both types.

More difficult to explain is the small shield, or whatever else it may be, which is worn on the hips, on Pls. II. and III., not only by the musicians and charioteers, but also by the warriors already provided with large shields. It appears to be attached to a girdle or *zoster*, and would thus be capable of being moved round to the front of the body or the back, as danger suggested in actual war, the hips not being vulnerable. Such a movement would answer to the term οἰηκίζειν, literally "to steer," which Herodotus[3] employs to describe the primitive shields of the Carians before they had invented the ὄχανα or handles by which they carried the shield on the left arm. It is true that he expressly says that these primitive shields were slung round the neck, and his description may very well apply to the large square shields seen on the primitive "island gems" of the Mycenæan age.[4] But it may equally hold good of this hitherto unknown piece of armour. In another passage Herodotus,[5] when speaking of the Scythian kings, says that they wore a golden *phialè* attached to

---

[1] Loeschcke, *Jahrb.* 1887, p. 277. In reference to the two riders on these vases, it is impossible to overlook the nude girls riding on huge horses which occur on our fragmentary vases from Defenneh, and on which the Ionian element is strongly pronounced, as I had suggested in *Tanis* II., p. 70, where one of these fragments is given, pl. 29. It was subsequently published in colours, *Ant. Denkmäler*, ii. pl. 21, fig. 2. My impression is that these nude girls on horseback must represent some funeral custom in Asia Minor. Lucian, *Charon*,

13, speaking of the Scythian Queen, Tomyris, says: ὁρᾷς τὴν Σκυθίδα τὴν ἐπὶ τοῦ ἵππου τούτου τοῦ λευκοῦ ἐξελαύνουσαν.

[2] Kinkel, *Epic. Gr. Frag.* i. p. 268, αὐτὰρ ὕπερθεν ἵππων δαρτὰ πρόσωπ' ἐφάρειν ἐσκληκότα καπνῷ. M. Joubin, *Bull. Corr. Hell.* 1895, p. 85, compares the helmet of Odysseus, *Iliad*, x. 263, on the outside of which were white boar's tusks.

[3] i. 171.

[4] Reichel, *Homer. Waffen*, p. 33.

[5] iv. 70.

the *zoster* at the place of fastening, ἐπὶ ἄκρης τῆς συμβολῆς, with which we may perhaps compare the phrase of Horace, " Natis in usum lætitiæ scyphis | pugnare Thracum est " (Car. I. 27). The metal disc on our sarcophagus is not unlike a *phialè*. But perhaps more to the point is the warrior on our very archaic Lycian *soros*,[1] who both carries a large circular shield on his left arm and holds up with his right hand a smaller disc or targe. We are aware of the difficulties which surround the Homeric *zoster* and *mitrè*, otherwise it would be tempting to suggest that this new piece of armour might assist in solving the problem.[2] Be this as it may, the rest of the armour on our sarcophagus is manifestly subsequent to the time when the Carians introduced their three famous improvements of a crest, handles for their shields and devices for the same.

As regards the spears, provided with a σαυρωτήρ or butt-end, we have instances of the same on one of our fragmentary vases from Defennch.[3] The cuirass is in use, as are also the *laiseion*,[4] or pendant from the shield, and the greaves. The chariots are of the regular Ionian type, with Homeric wheels, κύκλα ὀκτάκνημα.[5] The huge swords of the Cimmerians and the action of striking downwards with them do not, so far as we have observed, find any exact parallel in Greek warfare. Such instances as we have noticed on the vases are associated with giants or oriental subjects. On the other hand, we know that among the Scythian peoples the sword was regarded as a god, and this is confirmed by Herodotus,[6] who says that an ancient iron sword placed on a mound served as an image of Ares, to which they offered sacrifices. Dio Chrysostom, on his visit to the Borysthenes, describes the friend who came to meet him on horseback as carrying a large sabre (μάχαιραν μεγάλην τῶν ἱππικῶν), and as wearing the anaxyrides with the rest of the Scythian costume.[7] On the head the Cimmerians wore *galeris incurvis*,[8] which answers to the head-gear on our sarcophagus and to other representations of this people, which need not here be specified. It is true that this head-gear does not alone absolutely differentiate them from certain tribes which we find among the Persians. None the less it is perfectly Scythian or Cimmerian, as is also the huge bow-case, gorytos.

There remains to be mentioned the head-gear of the charioteers and musicians on Pls. II.-III. These figures wear a close-fitting cap, which, from its being painted purple, may be taken to have been of bronze, that being the colour employed on the sarcophagus to indicate bronze. From an opening or the crown of the head a mass of hair escapes, carefully cut at the ends like a horse's tail. On the chariot frieze of the Mausoleum is preserved a youthful driver, having not only the robe, but also the long

---

[1] Perrot and Chipiez, v. p. 394, where, however, the disc held up in the right hand is much larger in proportion than in the sculpture.

[2] If Helbig (*Hom. Epos*², p. 290) is right in the example of a *mitrè* which he there gives, the step from it to our disc would not be great. Perrot and Chipiez, iv. p. 741, give a figure of a warrior with a buckler hanging from a belt round the neck, which recalls our sarcophagus.

[3] *Ant. Denkmäler*, i. pl. 46 ; *Jahrbuch*, 1895, p. 40. Aristotle, *Poetics*, xxvi. 14, referring to the dispute concerning the arms of Achilles, quotes,

ἔγχεα δέ σφιν ὀρθ᾽ ἐπὶ σαυρωτῆρος, adding, "so it was then the custom as it is now among the Illyrians."

[4] Reichel, *Homer. Waffen*, p. 65.

[5] Studniczka, *Jahrbuch*, 1890, p. 147.

[6] iv. 62. Cf. Ammianus Marcellinus, xxxi. 2, 23, who says that they had no temples nor huts, " sed gladius barbarico ritu humi figitur nudus eumque ut Martem . . . colunt."

[7] *Orat.* xxxvi.

[8] Ammianus Marcellinus, xxxi. 2, 5.

hair of a girl. At present we are ignorant of the origin of this curious custom of dressing up boys, and even men, in female attire when they appeared in certain public competitions. Possibly it had been Ionian. At all events this peculiar treatment of the hair has been noticed as occurring not only on the sarcophagi of Clazomenæ, but also in some other instances where Ionian influence is unmistakable, as on a fragment of a vase from Naucratis and a hydria from Civita Castellana, both of which are in the British Museum.[1] It does not seem that the expression ὄπιθεν κομόωντες, which Homer[2] employs for the Abantes, need here apply. Possibly it would be more appropriate to cite a well-known passage of Athenæus,[3] where the Samians are described as celebrating the festival of Hera, κατεκτενισμένοι τὰς κόμας ἐπὶ τὸ μετάφρενον καὶ τοὺς ὤμους. But the most exact parallel we can find is a group of Egyptian girls[4] engaged in gymnastic exercises, whose hair is seen fastened at the crown and then escaping in a square-cut mass. The only difference is that the crown of the head is not there covered with a cap, as on the sarcophagus.

Fig. 3 reproduces the two remaining parallel bands on the cover of the sarcophagus. On the upper band we recognise a central combat over a fallen warrior. On each side stands a warrior looking on. Next on the right an armed man holds up his hand to arrest the advance of the chariots towards the centre. Beside the first chariot a man holds up a whip to the driver, while the hero steps up into the chariot leading by the wrist a woman-captive, who, it is noticeable, also wears her hair escaping in a tail at the crown of

---

[1] B. 59 (*Vase Catalogue*, ii. pl. 2), and B. 103, 14 (3). Studniczka, *Jahrbuch*, 1896, p. 268. *Cf.* the fragments of sarcophagi published by Dennis in the *Hellenic Journal*, iv. p. 5.

[2] *Iliad*, ii. 542.

[3] xii. 30. *Cf.* the fragment of Asius on the same subject (Kinkel, *Epic. Gr. Frag.* i. p. 206). Polyaenus, *Strat.* i. 23, says that the Samians went armed to the temple of Hera.

[4] *Rosellini*, ii. pl. 101, fig. 3 : *cf.* Krause, *Plotina*, pl. 3, figs. 33[a,b,c]. There is no possible question of the hair being shorn on the sarcophagus, as is the case of the African tribe mentioned by Herodotus, iv. 175 : οἱ λόφους κείρονται, τὸ μὲν μέσον τῶν τριχῶν ἀνίεντες αὔξεσθαι τὸ δὲ ἔνθεν καὶ ἔνθεν κείροντες ἐν χροΐ. Nor of the kind of pig-tail which Mr. Flinders Petrie calls the Libyan lock, *Hellenic Journal*, xi. p. 275.

FIG. 3.

the head like the charioteers and musicians elsewhere. Behind follow a man with horse and a chariot. On the lower band it [seems impossible to make out more than that it is a battle.

On a technical point it may here be remarked that the interior panels, Pls. II.–III. and Pls. IV.–V., resemble each other so closely as to suggest at first sight that they might have been executed by some mechanical process in the nature of a stencil plate, such as Theodoric[1] is said to have used in signing his name. But on closer examination there are too many small varieties of detail to allow of this in any true sense. What is probable is that the painter had before him an exact sketch of certain of the groups and figures, which he set himself to reverse and reduplicate as occasion offered. In the centre of Pl. II. the warrior moving away to the left seems to carry his shield wrongly on the right arm, thus exposing the inside of the shield, which is precisely what would happen in reversing the corresponding warrior on the right. It is therefore fairly conclusive that the painter had reproduced the one figure by simply reversing the other. The mistake of placing a shield on the right arm is so extraordinary that this alone would justify the suspicion that a mechanical process of reversing the figures had been employed. In any case it is certain that in both these figures it is the inside of the shield which is shown. Add to this the general correspondence which pervades Pls. II. and III and Pls. IV. and V. We shall then hardly escape the conclusion that the artist has had before him only a limited number of figures or groups, which he has, in a more or less free manner, reversed and reduplicated.

On the upper edge of the body of the sarcophagus (Pl. VI.) are a series of chariot races to which we have already referred. The two long sides correspond with each other so far as they have been preserved; apparently this had also been the case with the two short ends, though one of these has been much defaced. It is noticeable that on the two short ends the designs have been placed so as to be seen from one point of view, and thus seem to indicate the head and the foot of the sarcophagus.

On the under edge of the cover is a design which we give under Pl. VII. The main part is a battle scene. Above this are two groups of Odysseus and Ajax slaying Dolon, the one group being a simple repetition of the other without even the reversing of the attitude of Dolon, which would have been expected. Immediately above are two groups of two Sphinxes confronted, each group being a reversal of the other. These Sphinxes have each a long curl escaping at the crown of the head, as on the Sphinxes on the pottery from Naucratis, and on objects in gold and ivory from the Mycenæan tombs of Enkomi in Cyprus.[2] Higher up have been preserved a group of two Harpies and a man beside a horse. It will be observed that the Harpies resemble those on the Harpy tomb in having human arms and egg-shaped bodies, which apparently was the more archaic manner of representing them.

---

[1] Ammianus Marcellinus, *excerpta*, 79, laminam auream jussit interrasilem fieri, quattuor litteras regis habentem, Theod., ut si subscribere voluisset, posita lamina super chartam per eam penna duceret et subscripto ejus tantum videretur.

[2] Compare the gold ornament from Cyprus in the *Revue Arch.*, 1897 (xxxi.), p. 333.

At each end the cover takes the form of a pediment, having within it a painted group. At the one end (see Fig. 4), on each side of a central column, is a man running beside a horse inwards towards the column; while in an upper field of the design,

FIG. 4.

separated by a broad mæander border, are two figures also running inwards towards the column. In the opposite pediment (Fig. 5) is a central column between two Centaurs who appear to be attacking each other, armed with a branch of a tree, but this group is very much destroyed.

The shape and dimensions of our sarcophagus are indicated in Figs. 1 and 2, but, as this is the first instance in which a cover has been found among the sarcophagi of Clazomenæ, we may cite, as a sort of prototype, the two terra-cotta urns which were discovered in Crete some years ago.[1] These also have covers, with sloping roofs, on which patterns of the Mycenæ kind are painted. At the other extreme, in point of time, we have the Alexander sarcophagus from Sidon, and, as a variation, the Lycian

FIG. 5.

tombs, with sculptured designs along the roof and in the pediments. But there is this difference, that the top edge of our sarcophagus and the under edge of the cover have been elaborately decorated with paintings, which must have been entirely concealed from view when the cover was finally placed in position.

From a technical point of view, the production of these two huge masses of painted terra-cotta must have involved extraordinary skill. The sarcophagus was found broken in many pieces, and from the fractures we see that it had been first constructed in very thick masses of a rough terra-cotta with which pounded brick had been mixed, such as now goes by the

[1] *Mon. Ant. dei Lincei*, i. pl. 1, p. 201.

name of "pot-earth." At this stage the body and the cover would each be slightly fired (biscuit). The next stage was to cover the whole with a thin coating of fine clay, upon which the various mouldings were impressed, probably from wood moulds. After this the whole surface, both of body and cover, received a very thin white slip, upon which, when it was dry, the figured designs and the patterns were executed in a colour which, under firing, would become a black glaze. Meantime upon this black colour the painter had added his numerous details of white and purple. We understand from men of the greatest practical experience that the firing had most probably been effected by building a kiln round the sarcophagus, and that this firing had been at a low temperature, extending probably from four to six weeks. As regards the present effect of the colours, it is noticeable that in the interior the designs (Pls. II. and IV.), with their two counterparts, Pls. III. and V., are quite red, while the patterns on the exterior are in parts black, in other parts shading off rapidly into red. On the cover there is very little trace of this change of colour under firing. The designs are almost continuously black upon white, which possibly was the original intention, notwithstanding the charming effect of colour which the interior presents with its red figures against a white ground.

Last year, M. Salomon Reinach, in discussing the eighteen sarcophagi from Clazomenæ known to him at that time, arrived at the conclusion that they all belonged to a date anterior to B.C. 540. So far as we can see, our sarcophagus introduces no new elements which would assist in defining its date more precisely, unless the Cimmerian invasion may serve as a reason for carrying the date backwards, nearer to B.C. 600.

SARCOPHAGUS FROM CAMEIROS.

Pl. VIII.

B ETWEEN 1860 and 1864 the Museum made several important purchases of antiquities from MM. Salzmann and Biliotti, the fruit of their excavations among the tombs of Cameiros in Rhodes. The most extensive of these purchases was that of 1864. In one respect it was also the most important, because these antiquities were accompanied by a careful and detailed Diary of the Excavations, compiled by Mr., now Sir Alfred, Biliotti, describing the contents of each tomb as it was opened. Unfortunately we possess no similar record of the previous acquisitions. We are told nothing of the finding of the sarcophagus now before us, nor of a series of vases painted in the same manner, which also were acquired previous to 1864. The probability is that a careful account had been kept of the earlier excavations also, and that it had been reserved by M. Salzmann among his papers with a view to his projected work, the *Nécropole de Camiros*, the plates of which appeared in 1875. He, however, did not live to issue the text, nor have we been told in what state of preparation he had left it.

It is known that a series of gold ornaments acquired by the Museum in 1861 from this source, and familiar because of their figures of the so-called Artemis Persikè and winged bulls, had been found in a tomb with a large porcelain scarab of Psammetichos (B.C. 666-612). In addition to this express statement there is a letter from Mr. Vice-Consul (afterwards Sir Charles) Newton, dated Oct. 1, 1859, stating that when in Rhodes he had examined the antiquities which had been found by Messrs. Salzmann and Biliotti, and were then being offered to the Museum for purchase. The letter proceeds to specify some of the objects in detail as follows :—

" 1. A pair of pendants for earrings, ornamented with winged bulls, embossed in relief, and picked out with filagree [granulated patterns ?]. The style of these bulls is very Assyrian, but perhaps it would be more exact to say Phoenician.

" 2. A number of pendants of earrings, embossed with a figure, perhaps intended to represent the sun-god, with a *nimbus* round the head. These pendants are in quite a different style from the preceding, and seem to be executed under Egyptian influence.

" 3. A necklace from the centre of which hangs a bull's head as pendant. This rather resembles in style the pendants No. 1.

" The interest of these gold ornaments is much enhanced by the fact that they were found in the same graves with the vases which are chiefly of the class known as Nolan-Egyptian, or Phoenician, the subjects being animals and monsters painted in brown and crimson on a cream-coloured ground, *semé* with flowers. Among the vases is a series of pinakes, or platters, remarkable for their size and the freshness and beauty of their designs. One in particular deserves notice as a specimen of early drawing. The picture represents a Sphinx."

So far as concerns the last-mentioned vase (pinax representing a Sphinx, now in Brit. Mus., A. 745), it is obvious that the figure of the Sphinx has been executed in exactly the same manner as the animals on the sarcophagus. And if we could be sure that this vase had actually been found in a tomb with gold ornaments of the time of Psammetichos, we should then have absolute certainty as to the date of this particular method of painting on terra-cotta, instead of only an extreme degree of probability such as is now generally accepted.

On the other hand, it appears from a consular note of Sir Charles Newton, of the same year (1859), that he classified the vases found up to then by MM. Salzmann and Biliotti as falling into four categories:—(1) Vases of the class brought by Lord Elgin from Athens, and now known as of the geometric and Dipylon style. Of these the Museum acquired several important specimens from Cameiros on that occasion. (2) Vases with subjects painted in black and crimson, with *incised* lines on a cream-coloured ground. The incised lines, like the "field *semé* with flowers" above quoted, would, if taken literally, point to a stage of painting later than the sarcophagus and its kindred vases. (3) Vases which he describes as of the style called "affected Tyrrhenian," having black figures, with incised lines on a red ground. (4) Vases in a conventional style, thought to be an imitation of the archaic. In this style the figures are painted in black, with accessories in crimson and white with incised lines. This class of vases we have never seen except from Italy, where they are found in great abundance. The explanation of this difference between the consular note and the letter may be this, that in the note the whole of the vases are classed in these four categories, while in the letter only those are specified which were found with the gold ornaments. On this view the pottery of the Dipylon style to which he refers could be regarded as having come from older tombs, the vases of the third and fourth categories from later tombs. That would be in harmony with what is otherwise known of the development of vase painting. On the other hand, there is always, and nowhere more so than at Cameiros, the possibility of an extensive overlapping of different archaic styles of painting, and in particular the continuance of a primitive style of pottery side by side with a more advanced style. It is necessary to lay stress on this point, because in the Diary of Excavations of 1864 we find that on the site called Papas Loures by Biliotti, the results derived from the sixteen tombs there opened point consistently to a late stage of the Dipylon period. Yet from these tombs were obtained an oenochoe identical in technique with the sarcophagus and a kylix (A. 698), with conventional faces of lions executed in the same manner. In the tomb with the oenochoe (bands of goats and deer) nothing else survived. In the tomb with the kylix the following objects:—(1) Part of a large vase painted with figures of Centaurs and patterns of the Dipylon class (A. 439). (2) A fragmentary cup of red ware with geometric patterns incised. (3) Part of a vase similar to last. (4) A number of bronze fibulae of a geometric type (Catalogue of Bronzes, Figs. 7-9). (5) Glass beads. (6) Rosettes of pale gold. From these circumstances it is reasonable to conclude that the geometric and Dipylon systems of vase decoration, consisting in the main of patterns of a geometric order, with animals and human figures in secondary parts, had in Rhodes at least survived for a time side by side with the subsequent Asiatic system, in which animals assume the leading parts, and patterns are relegated to secondary places.

The peculiar phase of painting on terra-cotta to which we have referred as characteristic of this sarcophagus, has of late years attracted much attention from specialists in this department of archæology, each seeking to arrive at a definite classification, and all coming to more or less the same conclusion. The latest, and at the same time one of the best qualified, is M. Pottier.[1] With Pl. VIII. before us we shall be able to follow his classification of the Rhodian technique so far as concerns the three methods which he distinguishes in it:—(1) The representation of the head and sometimes the paws of an animal by means of painted lines, which he truly says is a very ancient method, dating back even to the Mycenæan age. (2) The representation of the body of the animal as an opaque silhouette, but with the inner lines which mark the anatomy of the animal *vacant* (traits réservés) on the ground colour of the vase, a process which, he adds, makes its first appearance when the Dipylon style of vase-painting began to develop into new fields. As, however, both these methods are invariably combined on the vases in question, it would be an advantage if one term could be found which would describe them both. It is, in fact, the same combination of drawing and painting with which we are confronted on the Cameiros sarcophagus and the kindred vases. (3) His third method, the substitution of incised for vacant or left lines, only concerns us here in so far as the presence of this method is an indication of the stage of painting which followed immediately upon that of our sarcophagus. It is, however, of some importance to note that both these methods (2 and 3) are combined on a sarcophagus from Clazomenae, which has recently been acquired for America.

It will be seen from Pl. VIII. that the animals on the Cameiros sarcophagus present an obvious combination of the first two methods described by M. Pottier, that is to say, the heads of the animals are in each case examples of line drawing with a brush, while the bodies are painted in with a full brush. Certain inner lines indicating anatomical structure are left to show in the white ground of the vase, while in the case of the bull a large patch of the white ground represents the piebald colour of the creature. In the lions the feet and lower part of the legs are filled in with colour and not drawn in line.

In this strange combination of drawing and painting we are struck with the amount of care which must have been necessary in painting round the inner lines, so as to leave them reserved or vacant, especially so on the kindred vases, where the figures of animals are much smaller than on the sarcophagus. In the subsequent stage of the art these lines were by a much simpler process painted in with white over the black colour with which the whole body of the animal was first laid in. What the origin of the earlier and more laborious process may have been has not been explained. But taking into consideration that the larger the figures, the more easy would this method be, we may perhaps assume that it had been derived from painting on a large scale. In view of this suggestion we may refer to the painted slabs of terra-cotta from Caere

[1] *Catalogue des Vases Antiques du Louvre*, 1896, p. 145. Compare his article in the *Monuments Piot*, i. p. 45, where he publishes a Rhodian vase on which are combined the two methods of *vacant* and of *incised* lines, as on a vase now in Berlin (*Hellen. Journ.* 1885, p. 186, fig. 3), and on a large lebes from Naucratis in the Brit. Mus. (A. 957), which latter was apparently unknown to M. Pottier.

now in the British Museum, on which the system of reserved or vacant lines is conspicuous, and as to which there can be little doubt that these slabs represent a method of painting derived from Asia Minor.[1]

In the passage referred to above M. Pottier recognises the practice of line drawing with a brush as common also to the Mycenæ period. It is, in fact, a conspicuous feature of the so-called Mycenæan vases. We may add that on at least one well-known vase from Ialysos (of the Mycenæ style), the figure is filled in with black, while the inner lines are reserved on the white ground.[2] That is to say, the method of painting is exactly the same as on the Cameiros sarcophagus, on a series of Cameiros vases, on several fine vases from Naucratis, and on others from Daphnae in Egypt; while again on other vases of the Mycenæ class is to be seen the later and more rapid method of putting in the inner lines with white over the black colour.[3] In the warrior-vase of Mycenæ,[4] in its companion (the vase signed by the potter Aristonophos in Rome), and in vases of the Melos group, we find a more ambitious stage of the art, when human figures and even legendary scenes become prominent. But the method of combining drawing with painting and of reserving the inner lines remains in force, if indeed somewhat degenerate. So that on the whole it would appear as if the immediate antecedents of the Cameiros sarcophagus and its congeners had been vases of the Mycenæ period. How long antecedent they were is the question which yet remains to be determined.[5]

Meantime it is agreed on all hands that the earliest geometric or Dipylon style of vase painting was followed immediately in Attica with figures of animals in which the combination of drawing and painting just described is the conspicuous feature. It is believed that this change was due to an impulse derived from the importation or knowledge of vases of the Cameiros, Naucratis and Daphnae class, as specified above. An excellent illustration may be seen in the Burgon lebes (A. 535), having two large figures of lions standing confronted. There is, however, this difference, that neither on the Burgon lebes, nor on any other vases of its class, have we observed the existence of these laboriously reserved inner lines, which lend so marked a character to the vases we have referred to from Cameiros,[6] Naucratis,[7] and Daphnae.[8] In the circumstances the omission of these lines was to be expected, on the principle that in imitation it is mainly the general effect that is aimed at.

On the vases in question from Naucratis there occurs frequently the figure of a Sphinx having a sort of tendril projecting from the crown of the head. The same

[1] *Journal of Hellenic Studies*, x. pl. 7, and pp. 244-245 and 248-249.

[2] Furtwaengler and Loeschcke, *Mykenische Vasen*, pl. 1, fig. 1.

[3] Cuttle-fish from Ialysos in Furtwaengler and Loeschcke, *Myk. Vasen*, pl. 8, fig. 49.

[4] Furtwaengler and Loeschcke, *Myk. Vasen*, pls. 42-43.

[5] F. Dümmler, in *Jahrbuch*, 1891, p. 270, says: " Da es jetzt wahrscheinlich ist dass mykenische Keramik in Argolis bis gegen 800 v. Chr. geherrscht hat, würde sich der rhodische Stil direkt aus dem mykenischen haben entwickeln können unter Mitwirkung verschiedenen fremdartigen Imports, ohne dass in Argolis selbst ein geometrischer Stil zwischen dem mykenischen und rhodischen bestanden hätte."

[6] For Cameiros specimens see the oenochoae in *Vases Antiques du Louvre*, pl. 12.

[7] *Naucratis*, pt. 1. pl. 4, and pt. 11. pls. 5-6. On the lebes on pl. 8 the upper row of animals has the inner lines incised, while the lower row has them vacant.

[8] *Tanis* II., pls. 27-28.

characteristic is to be seen still in force on the Clazomenæ sarcophagus, and, tracing the feature backward in point of time, we meet it again on the gold ornaments from Enkomi, in Cyprus, found in tombs with Mycenæan vases. It will be seen also from the Cameiros sarcophagus that the piebald colour of the bull is rendered in the same manner as on the painted bull from Tiryns and on fragments of vases from Mycenæ.[1] As the striking resemblance in these instances cannot have been casual we must suppose that it had been the result of a common method of painting and a common tradition, however separated the individual objects may have been in time. It does not follow that this method had originated in Rhodes or in Asia Minor. But the fact is not to be ignored that the discovery of sarcophagi at Clazomenæ has of late years confirmed in an extraordinary manner the classical tradition of an early school of painting in Asia Minor. For the present we cannot trace this school beyond the Clazomenæ stage further back than to the stage of the Cameiros sarcophagus. But that of itself must mean a certain distance of time.

It remains now to describe the Cameiros sarcophagus in detail. To begin with, when set upright on end, it has the appearance of a doorway, not unlike the door of the peribolos, or enclosing wall, of the Heröon at Giölbaschi, in Lycia,[2] the sculptures of which are now in Vienna. Apparently the intention in both cases had been to suggest the portal of Hades, through which the deceased would have to pass. In later times the most usual form of a Greek stelè, or tombstone, was that of a doorway, and that this was meant for the portal of Hades is now evident from a terra-cotta vase recently acquired by the Museum, on which is represented, in relief, the Rape of Persephonè. In front of the chariot of Hades is a stelè, inscribed ϵϜϴϵϵΝϴ, and beyond it the reeds of Acheron and the Danaides filling in vain their pitchers. The stelè, therefore, indicates the entrance to Hades.

On the head of the sarcophagus is a bull standing to the left between two lions confronted, and having their faces turned round full to the front. The heads of the lions are rendered in lines, but it is noticeable that this method of drawing is not extended to the lower part of their legs, as in the vases referred to from Cameiros and Naucratis. This omission may be taken as an indication of a somewhat later date for the sarcophagus. Still more suggestive of a later date is the drawing of the lions' heads full to the front instead of in profile, implying, as it does, an increased dexterity and a new desire towards vividness of representation. On the other hand, the two lions back to back on the foot of the sarcophagus have their heads drawn in profile, like the vases in question, and only differ from the vases in the more strictly heraldic grouping of the animals, reminding us in this respect of the two lions on the Burgon lebes of the later Dipylon style. The breadth of manner and fine sweep of lines with which the bull and the two lions at the head of the sarcophagus are painted far exceed the work on the vases, and prepare us for the two heads of warriors immediately beneath. Nothing comparable to the severe and refined aspect of these two heads has been found in the vase painting of this period. They point rather to a higher walk of art, in which the

---

[1] Furtwaengler and Loeschcke, *Myken. Vasen,* pl. 41. Cf. Brunn, *Gr. Kunstgeschichte,* p. 45.

[2] Collignon. *Hist. de la Sculpt. Grecque,* ii. p. 205.

Greek ideal had already begun to assert itself in no insignificant manner. In style they recall the heads of the two warriors found by Prof. Ramsay on a rock-cut tomb in Phrygia.[1]

In speaking of the *heraldic* grouping of the lions, we have used a convenient term. The meaning is that one lion is almost as much a counterpart of the other as if it had been made from a reversed tracing. Apparently the result which we are now describing as heraldic was nothing more than a piece of artistic economy, such as we saw carried out on a large scale on the Clazomenæ sarcophagus. It is a sort of *compendiaria*, or short-cut, though possibly a very different compendiaria from that which Petronius[2] says had been invented by the audacity of the Egyptians, involving, he says, the inevitable decline of the art of painting.

In the foregoing discussion it has been necessary to give a number of details. But the purpose in view has been to show, or at all events to suggest, that the Cameiros sarcophagus was artistically a descendant of an earlier stage of painting in Asia Minor which had been more or less closely related to the vase painters of the Mycenæan period, on the one hand, and to those of the Asiatic and Dipylon periods on the other.

The sarcophagus was acquired in 1863. Its dimensions are: Length, 6 feet 5 in.; width at top, 2 ft. 1 in.; at bottom, 1 foot 11 in. The clay is covered with a white slip, upon which the figures and patterns are painted exclusively in black. Partly published in Salzmann's *Nécropole de Camiros*, pl. 1, figs. 1–2.

---

[1] *Journal of Hellen. Studies*, ix. p. 363.
[2] *Satirae*, 2: Pictura quoque non alium exitium fecit, postquam Ægyptiorum audacia tam magnae artis compendiariam invenit.

SARCOPHAGUS FROM CAERE.

Pls. IX.—XI.

IN the Papa Giulio Museum at Rome there has recently been acquired from Caere a terra-cotta sarcophagus, having on the lid a group of a man and woman reclining together. In point of artistic style this sarcophagus may be assigned to about the same date as the specimen in the British Museum here published, though the details are more minutely finished and the style somewhat more refined in the one at Rome. On the other hand, it has no reliefs nor any decoration on the body of the sarcophagus. In the Louvre there has long been on exhibition another Etruscan sarcophagus in terra-cotta, having a similar group of a man and woman reclining on the lid in much the same archaic manner, but again without any reliefs on the body of the sarcophagus.[1] The Louvre specimen is richly coloured.

These three sarcophagi, though differing in point of style and execution, appear to be more or less contemporary, the differences of style and execution being due probably to the idiosyncrasies of Etruscan artists working under the foreign influence of Greek art. To this question it will be necessary to return; meanwhile all three have this in common, that they present us with the earliest known type of a group of two reclining figures on the lid of a sarcophagus. That is a phenomenon with which we are familiar in later Etruscan and in Roman art. It can now be traced back to near 600 B.C. But what was its origin?

The idea, doubtless, is that of a man and woman reclining at a banquet, as we see them in the archaic painted tombs of the Etruscans, and, indeed, on the reliefs of the Museum sarcophagus (Pl. X.). Apparently the group on the lids of the sarcophagi has been simply abstracted from one of those scenes of funeral banquets; but the frequency of these scenes in early Etruscan art is not sufficient to prove that the origin of the idea was Etruscan. There was a time when it might have seemed so, but the finding of a number of terra-cotta sarcophagi at Clazomenae has opened up a new possibility, the issue of which time alone can show.

Assuming, as it seems fair to do, that the group in the round on our sarcophagus was derived from the older conception of a similar group in relief or in painting, we have next to consider the difficulties of the situation. These life-size figures had to be

[1] *Mon. dell' Inst.* vi. pl. 59 ; *Annali*, 1861, p. 390 ; *Musée Napoleon III.* pl. 80. In the British Museum is a terra-cotta urn in the shape of a small sarcophagus having an effigy of a female lying on the lid, while on the front of it is a narrow band of reliefs representing a central group of two lions attacking a bull, with a Satyr reclining at each end.

made hollow. It was necessary that the clay should contain a minimum of moisture, so as to avoid the dangers of expansion or contraction during the firing. Apparently the figures had been modelled over an inner core of wood, which under the process of firing would gradually disappear. In one place the chances and changes of firing are very noticeable; the left foot of the man has shrunk to the extent of a good half inch in length. In the left hand of the man the upper joint of the thumb is on a line with the uppermost joints of the fingers, and as no one with any artistic training could have made such a mistake, we must conclude that it also has been due to some mischance in the firing. It was in antiquity a matter for surprise when a terra-cotta chariot group at Veii had in the firing burst the kiln asunder. The Augurs proclaimed that Veii would successfully resist the Romans so long as it held to that sarcophagus. But the incident, though it may have been extraordinary, could not have been altogether unexpected among a people so well accustomed to working in terra-cotta as were the ancient Etruscans.

The reliefs on the sides of the sarcophagus were not subject to the same danger. The process was different. The four sides would be erected first in pounded brick or potter's earth, from which the moisture would be extracted by a preliminary firing. There would next be laid on a thin surface coating of finer clay, on which the reliefs would be stamped from moulds; then would follow the painting, and a final firing at a low heat.

At this point it may be interesting to compare a somewhat older work of Etruscan art, the bronze bust from the Polledrara tomb in the British Museum (B.C. 666-612), for the sake of the striking contrast which is presented between the reliefs round the base of the bust, and the artistic aspect of the bust itself. The reliefs exhibit many of the excellences which arise from an art that has been practised for some time, while the bust itself betrays in a glaring manner an inexperience in working in the round. In a less degree, as would be expected in a more advanced stage of art, our sarcophagus furnishes the same contrast between its reliefs and its figures in the round.

Bearing in mind the difficulties that beset the sculptor of a life-sized group of terra-cotta, in particular the difficulty of translating from relief into the round, we are prepared to expect in the man and woman on our sarcophagus a strong measure of realism. The decorative instinct which had been developed in the reliefs was no longer available. The figures must be as nearly as possible life-like, subject always to the artistic traditions and conventions of the age, which could not be broken through. Sir C. T. Newton said[1] with perfect truth :—

"The style of these figures is archaic, the treatment throughout very naturalistic, in which a curious striving after truth in anatomical details gives animation to the group, in spite of the extreme ungainliness of form and ungraceful composition."

In the man the evidence of realism is most apparent in the modelling of the torso. Hardly any trace of convention or tradition remains. In the limbs, however, there is less of this direct study of nature, while again the face is simply a mask, executed on traditional lines. We see that it is a mask from the artificial rendering of the hair over the forehead, and are reminded thereby of the use of such masks to cover the faces of

[1] *Castellani Collection*, p. 5, pls. 18-20; compare Dennis, *Cities and Cemeteries of Etruria*,[1] i. p. 281.

the dead in early times, as, for example, in the gold masks of Mycenæ and other instances.[1] As regards the face of the woman, there is no such direct proof that it also is a mask, and no inference can be made one way or the other so long as it is unknown whether she is to be regarded as living or dead.

The body of the woman is strongly naturalistic. In a rough general manner the forms under the drapery are made to express themselves forcibly. The drapery has to give up much of its older conventionalisms and has not yet found a proper substitute for them, whereas the thicker drapery over the legs retains fully the old conventions. On the other hand, the feet and ankles again make a considerable show of realism. It is noticeable that she wears sandals, under which are thin stockings. Shoes, or even high boots, may have been more in accordance with early Etruscan usage; but the instances of sandals are numerous enough. The point for the moment is, that in the other archaic examples the feet and the sandals alike adhere to a strictly conventional type, while on our sarcophagus the feet of the woman seem almost to feel the rude touch of the rough straps of the sandals. The thin stocking accentuates that sense of touch. For the rest, we know of no other example of stockings among the remains of ancient art.

In the reliefs on the sides of the sarcophagus there was no specially new problem to be solved. The art of working in relief in terra-cotta had already passed through its apprenticeship, and had established certain fixed types for individual figures, and for a limited range of compositions. Its method of repeating figures and groups from one and the same mould gave it an easy advantage for purposes of decoration. The Museum possesses a number of fragments from a terra-cotta frieze, apparently from a building of some sort, in which the same chariot group recurs four or five times. That is a process of artistic economy which we saw largely employed in the paintings of the sarcophagus from Clazomenæ. Even on the archaic limestone cistæ of the Etruscans the reliefs are sculptured in panels, as if under the direct influence of the terra-cotta method of working from moulds, so far as concerns their general form.

The question at the present day is, how far this method of working in relief in terra-cotta had been derived by the Etruscans from Greece or from Asia Minor, how long and to what extent that Hellenic influence had been exercised. Without entering on the details of this question, this much seems clear, that the Etruscans did possess a flourishing art of their own, even in times earlier than our sarcophagus. The proof of that is to be seen in the numerous wall-paintings on their tombs, the sculptured cistæ above referred to, and many objects of art of a portable kind in bronze or in gold. On the other hand, we see the archaic Etruscans employing the same alphabet as the contemporary Greeks, and find that their tombs have yielded vast numbers of painted vases and other examples of artistic luxury, which had obviously been imported from Greece, all testifying to a wide community of feeling between the two peoples during the archaic period. The difficulty is to establish a border line where these two classes of works of art appear to encroach the one upon the other. To take our sarcophagus

---

[1] Benndorf, *Gesichtshelme*, p. 70, pl. 11.

as an illustration, the group on the lid would come within the category of more or less purely Etruscan work, while the reliefs go to the opposite extreme of being dominated by the influence of Græce or of Asia Minor. At first sight there seems to be no detail in them which could not be found on the black-figure vases of the later Corinthian or Chalcidian class, while, on the other hand, there is an entire absence of strictly Etruscan costume, such as the pointed cap worn by Etruscan women, as we see them on the tomb paintings and the limestone cistæ. Yet on closer inspection there has been a general transformation, which pervades almost every detail. The girdles round the waists of the women and the borders of their dresses are exaggerated to a degree which has no parallel on the Greek vases, and can best be explained as examples of the form of exaggeration which usually attends the imitation of a foreign school of art.

In connection with these matters of fact we have to bear in mind certain traditions. We are told that the early art of Etruria had been greatly influenced by artists who had settled there in exile from Corinth, among them being the father of Tarquin. We know that in early times Corinth had been distinguished as a seat of working in terra-cotta. Corinth in its turn had been influenced by the art of Asia Minor, and of late years we have had abundant evidence in the sarcophagi of Asia Minor to show to what excellence the art of working in terra-cotta had there attained. Very possibly this art in passing through Corinth to Etruria had, at the same time, touched on other parts of Greece. But as yet the proofs in this direction are comparatively slight.

The subject of the reliefs has been thus described by Sir C. T. Newton[1]:—

" The relief on the front of the coffin represents a battle between two warriors, each attended by one male and two female figures. At either end of the scene is a winged figure. These probably represent the souls of the two warriors. On the opposite side of the coffin is represented a banquet at which a male and a female figure recline. At one end are two warriors, each of whom appears to be taking leave of two female relatives. At the other end are two pairs of females, seated on chairs in a mourning attitude. It is to be presumed that the four scenes thus represented on the sides of the coffin have relation to one another, and that the four subjects represented are: the leave-taking of two warriors before going to single combat; the death of one of them; the mourning for that death; and the funeral feast, or possibly the reception of the slain warrior in the realms of bliss. But the particular single combat represented has not yet been identified. It should be noticed that in the single combat a lion is represented fastening on the leg of the falling warrior."

In the central group on the front the idea of a lion assisting a combatant is known elsewhere, as in the sculptures of Pergamon,[2] and again on the frieze of the Treasury of Knidos (?) discovered in the French excavations at Delphi, two or three years ago. In the example from Delphi we see the goddess Cybelè in the midst of a Gigantomachia driving a yoke of two lions, which seize upon a giant. Possibly some

[1] *The Castellani Collection*, p. 5.   [2] *Beschreibung*, p. 13.

similarly Asiatic legend of a warrior attended by a lion had found its way to Etruria. The only alternative that suggests itself is that the presence of the lion may have been meant to show by a species of anticipation or prolepsis that the body of the falling combatant was left to be devoured by wild beasts.

The explanation of the two winged figures at either end of the combat-scene as the souls of the warriors is justified by those instances of psychostasia, in which, as on an archaic vase in the Museum (B. 639), Hermes is seen weighing in a balance the souls of Achilles and Memnon during their encounter. It may be assumed that the soul of the wounded man is bounding off to Hades. The conception seems to be purely Greek, or more particularly Ionian Greek.

In the banquet scene on the back of the sarcophagus there appear certain vases on tall pedestals which correspond exactly in shape with a class of vases which have been found of late years at Falerii and elsewhere. These may be regarded as local Etruscan ware. It is noticeable also that one of the musicians carries a lyre in his hand of absurdly diminutive proportions. The shape of the lyre is correct, but its exceeding smallness implies that the artist was ignorant of the proportions of this instrument in Greek art, as an Etruscan artist might perhaps be excused for being, considering that the flutes were much more to his nature and practice.

The inscription on the front of the sarcophagus reads :[1]

> *Mivelaves' nas' mevepetursikipa*
> *Thaniavelaimatinainnata.*

The sarcophagus was acquired in 1873 from Alessandro Castellani, who in turn had purchased it from Pietro Pennelli. It reached the Museum in the condition in which it had been found at Caere (Cervetri)—that is to say, in a number of pieces, the fractured edges showing the same hard incrustation which is still visible on many parts of the surface. In ordinary circumstances it would be unnecessary even to mention, still less to emphasize, this condition of the sarcophagus when it arrived here, since nothing could be more satisfactory than the state of this terra-cotta.

It happened, however, that certain scholars took objection to the inscription on the ground of its resemblance to an Etruscan inscription on a gold fibula in the Louvre, and because of difficulties in explaining the structure of certain of the words. In a matter still so obscure as the Etruscan language, it was to be expected that while the most prominent of the then Etruscan scholars (Corssen) found no difficulty in the inscription, others would take a different view. As scholars they were entitled to do so, but when they proceeded to criticise the artistic features of the sarcophagus they forgot the advice of Apelles to his critic.

The sarcophagus measures 5 ft. 8 in. in height, inclusive of group, and 4 ft. 5 in. in length. It has been published by: Sir C. T. Newton, *The Castellani Collection* (1874), pls. 18-20 ; *Encyclopædia Britannica*, 9th ed., vol. 8, pl. 8 ; G. Dennis, *Cities and Cemeteries of Etruria*, 2nd ed., I. p. 227 and p. 280.

---

[1] See Deecke, *Etruskische Forschungen*, pt. 3, p. 257, where the literature of the subject is collected.

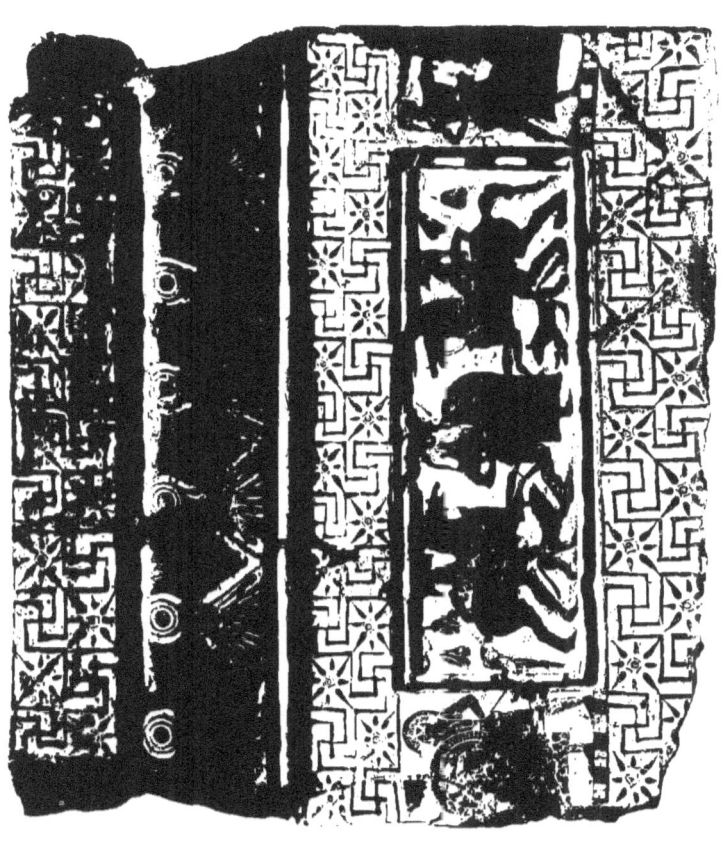

www.ingramcontent.com/pod-product-compliance
Lightning Source LLC
Chambersburg PA
CBHW031321280626
47169CB00019B/2580